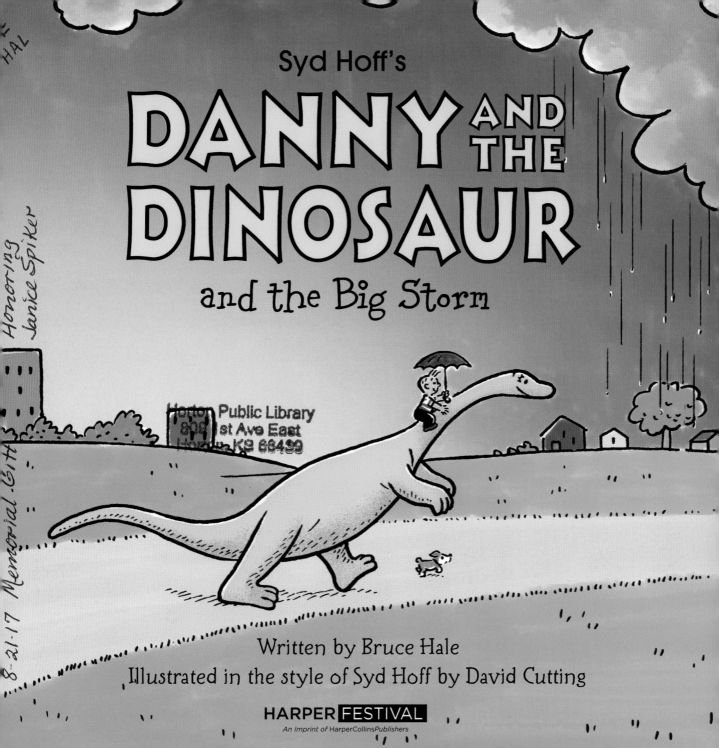

Syd Hoff's

DANNY AND THE DINOSAUR

and the Big Storm

Written by Bruce Hale

Illustrated in the style of Syd Hoff by David Cutting

HARPER FESTIVAL

An Imprint of HarperCollinsPublishers

HarperFestival is an imprint of HarperCollins Publishers.

Library of Congress Control Number: 2015958591
ISBN 978-0-06-241045-0

Book design and typography by Jeff Shake
16 17 18 19 20   SCP   10 9 8 7 6 5 4 3 2 1
❖
First Edition

The dinosaur was visiting Danny for a playdate. It was a beautiful
spring day. They played with the puppy and had a wonderful time.
But then the clouds rolled in, and . . .

...pitter-patter-pitter, it started to rain!
This wasn't so bad, until ...

... *BOOM! CRASH!* Thunder roared and it rained even harder.

"Don't worry," said Danny. "It's only a storm."

"Yipe!" the puppy whined, and ran indoors.
"YIKES!" the dinosaur cried, and joined her.

KA-BOOM! CRACKLE-CRASH! The lightning filled the sky and then thunder boomed.

The puppy jumped in fear.
But when the dinosaur jumped . . .

. . . he hit the ceiling!

"Ouch!" said the dinosaur.

"Oops. That's going to leave a mark," said Danny.

As lightning flashed again, the puppy ran and hid under the bed.

But when the dinosaur hid . . .

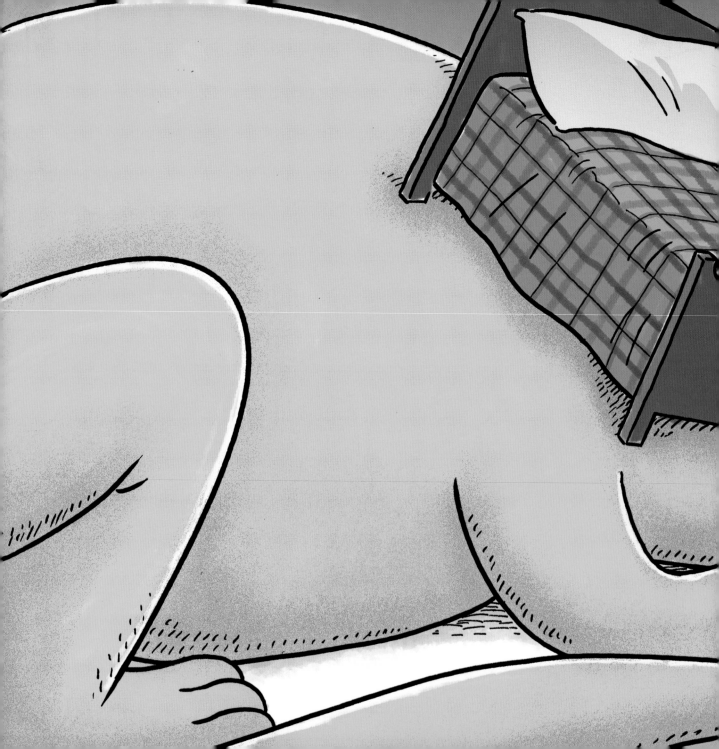

. . . things got a little bit crowded.

"Ow-ow-owoooo!" the puppy howled in fear at the storm.

"Easy now," said Danny. "It'll be all right."

When the dinosaur howled, "OW-WOOOO!" . . .

. . . Danny's parents came running to see what all the noise was about.
"We're a little bit scared of the storm," said Danny. "But it's almost passed."

He gave the puppy a hug,
and *she settled down.*

Everyone gave the dinosaur a hug, and he settled down, too.

And then the sun appeared. Danny, the dinosaur, and the puppy
ran outside to play. Soon all the neighborhood kids joined them.

They didn't even mind when the dinosaur stamped in the mud and got everyone muddy!

After all, it was *such* a beautiful day.